ROBERT D. SAN SOUCI

THE SNOW WIFE

Pictures by STEPHEN T. JOHNSON

Dial Books for Young Readers *New York*

Published by Dial Books for Young Readers
A Division of Penguin Books USA Inc.
375 Hudson Street
New York, New York 10014

Text copyright © 1993 by Robert D. San Souci
Pictures copyright © 1993 by Stephen T. Johnson
All rights reserved
Designed by Atha Tehon
Printed in the U.S.A.
First Edition
1 3 5 7 9 10 8 6 4 2

Library of Congress Cataloging in Publication Data
San Souci, Robert D.
The snow wife / by Robert D. San Souci; pictures by Stephen T. Johnson.
p.   cm.
Summary: When a Japanese woodcutter breaks his promise and
describes his encounter with a terrifying snow woman, he loses his
wife and must make a dangerous journey to win her back.
ISBN 0-8037-1409-2.—ISBN 0-8037-1410-6 (lib. bdg.)
[1. Folklore—Japan.] I. Johnson, Stephen, 1964–ill. II. Title.
PZ8.1.S227Sn   1993   [398.21]—dc20   92-28966   CIP   AC

*The full-color artwork was prepared
using watercolor and pastels.*

In memory of Yoshiko Uchida,
whose friendship was a gift to me
and whose writings were a gift to all of us
R. S. S.

For Debbie
S. T. J.

In Japan long ago there lived two woodcutters. Mosaku was an old man; Minokichi, his apprentice, had just turned eighteen.

One wintry evening the two men were returning from a distant forest to their village, when a terrible snowstorm overtook them. The winds howled like demons, pulling at their clothes and driving snow into their eyes.

Shaking from cold and nearly blind, they came upon a tiny hut. They knocked, but when no one answered, they went inside.

Although they were out of the wind, their wood was so wet they couldn't even start a fire.

"Oh, oh, oh!" cried old Mosaku, listening to the storm. "We will certainly freeze to death. I can feel the cold creeping under my skin."

"Don't give up," said Minokichi. "We can cover ourselves with our straw coats and huddle together."

When they had done this, Mosaku said, "I don't feel so cold any longer."

Soon after this the old man fell asleep. But Minokichi lay awake, listening to the roaring wind and the whisper of snow against the door. The hut swayed and creaked like a boat at sea. The room was growing even colder, and the young man shivered. In spite of the sounds and the bitter cold, though, he finally dozed off.

A burst of wind-driven snow in his face woke him. The door of the hut was wide open, and in the gray light he saw a woman with long black hair, dressed in a white kimono, bending over Mosaku, now clad only in his yellow robe. Her breath, like a cloud of bright white smoke, surrounded the sleeper's head.

Suddenly she turned to Minokichi. Although she was beautiful, the chilling look in her eyes frightened him. He tried to cry out, but his shout froze in his throat.

Her look quickly softened. For a long time she stared at the terror-stricken woodcutter, then she smiled and whispered, "You are young and handsome. I feel pity and something deeper for you. I will not harm you, nor will I forget you. But you must not tell anybody what you have seen, or you will suffer for it! Promise that you will never speak a word about me."

Able to find his voice at last, Minokichi whispered, "I promise, Merciful Lady."

Satisfied, the woman backed away from him and passed through the doorway. To his horror the woodcutter saw that she had no feet, but from the waist down was as mist, trailing away to a thread as thin as smoke from an extinguished candle. Then the door slammed shut behind her.

Still shivering from this strange meeting, he tried to rouse his friend Mosaku. But his companion was dead, his skin as cold as ice.

When the storm ended, Minokichi carried his poor friend back to the village, where he said only that Mosaku had died from the cold. He kept his promise and never spoke a word about the strange woman.

He now went alone to cut wood, and left the forest the moment snow began to fall. Often he had barely enough wood to sell in order to buy food. He thought himself fortunate that he was not yet married and had no family to support.

One evening the following winter as he was hurrying home laden with wood, he met a young woman traveling in the same direction. She was tall and slender and very pretty. When they exchanged polite greetings, Minokichi found her voice sweet and lilting.

"My name is Yuki," she said. The woodcutter thought it a perfect name, because *yuki* means "snow" and the woman's skin was as fair as freshly fallen snow. "I have lost both my parents, so I am going to the city to find work as a servant."

Charmed by her grace and beauty, Minokichi suddenly asked, "Are you married or promised to anyone?"

Yuki blushed, then laughed. "No. I am free. And you?"

This time it was the young man's turn to blush. "I am free also."

They talked of many things as they walked along. When they reached the village, it was very late. Minokichi arranged for Yuki to spend the night with a neighbor who was a widow.

As it turned out, Yuki never left the village. She and Minokichi fell in love and were soon married.

She was a good wife and mother to their two sons and a daughter. In spite of the passing years she looked as young and fresh as on the day her husband had first seen her.

One night, after she put the children to bed, Yuki sat sewing by the light of a paper lantern. Gazing at her, Minokichi said, "The way the lamplight catches your face reminds me of something very strange that happened the winter before we met."

Never lifting her eyes from her sewing, Yuki said, "What was that?"

"I met a woman almost as beautiful as you—but she was not human."

Yuki's needle had stopped, but still she did not look across the room at her husband. "Where did you meet her?"

Then Minokichi told her about the storm and Mosaku's death and the mysterious woman in white. "I have often wondered whether I really saw her," he ended, "or if I was only dreaming."

His wife flung aside her sewing, and stood up crying, "The woman you saw was I! You have broken your promise not to tell what you saw, and look what you have done!"

Even as he watched, Yuki was changing into the Woman of the Snow. "Oh, my poor little ones!" she wailed in a voice like a shrieking wind. Minokichi reached for her, but she became a white mist that swirled up to the roof and out the smoke hole. Overcome with remorse at his betrayal, he fell to his knees and wept through the night.

The next morning he went to the village priest, to ask if there was any way for him to bring back Yuki.

At first the priest tried to discourage Minokichi, saying, "A marriage between a human being and a spirit being is rarely a happy event. Accept your guilt and grief, and do not try to win back your snow wife."

"Our marriage was a good one," said the poor woodcutter, "and my children cry for their mother. I broke my promise. Finding Yuki is the only way I can ask to be forgiven."

"Very well," said the priest with a sigh. "Such spirits are ruled by the Wind God. You must journey to his shrine on the peak of Bitter Mountain and ask him to let her return to the world of humans. However, the way is dangerous and the temper of the Wind God is uncertain."

Although it was the coldest part of the winter, Minokichi left his children in the care of neighbors and set out through the cutting wind and stinging snow.

After many days of hard traveling he came to the slopes of Bitter Mountain. As he climbed the steep path edged with snow-laden pines, Minokichi came upon a Mountain Man huddled in the lee of a huge boulder. The creature, who was much shorter than Minokichi, resembled a great monkey covered with shaggy, reddish-brown fur.

"This path belongs to me," said the Mountain Man. "What will you give me to use it?"

"I am a poor woodcutter," explained Minokichi, bowing politely. "But I must visit the shrine at the mountain's top. All I have are some rice-balls in my pack."

"Give me half, and you may use the path. Refuse, and I'll chase you away." To prove how strong he was, the creature brushed the snow from a rock the size of a man's head, then squeezed the rock into dust that mingled with the drifting snow. Minokichi quickly handed over half his food, and the creature, gobbling noisily, waved him on his way.

Farther along the trail, the woodcutter found his way blocked by a Mountain Woman who sprang from a cave beside the path. Her body was covered with long, silky white hair. Sharp fangs jutted out of her mouth, and her eyes burned red. Minokichi came only up to her shoulder.

"This path belongs to me," she said. "Anyone I catch upon it must feed me to pay for trespassing."

"I have only some rice-balls," said Minokichi, "but I will share them with you."

The ogress laughed rudely. "I am hungry for something much better than rice."

"Alas! That is all I carry upon my person," he said.

"Your person is just the meal I desire!" roared the monster. Now Minokichi could see human bones scattered around the cave mouth behind her. The creature grabbed for him, but Minokichi eluded her. He hurried up the ice-slick path as fast as he could, the angry ogress lumbering along after him.

Quickly he pulled a rice-ball from his pocket. With the pin that fastened his coat, he stuck his finger, drawing a bead of blood. He dabbed this on the rice-ball and tossed it over his shoulder. The Mountain Woman paused to catch it and pop it into her mouth. Minokichi stumbled on, but all too soon he heard the ogress panting behind him.

Again he touched a rice-ball with a drop of blood and threw it after him, then a third and a fourth.

These delayed the monster long enough for Minokichi to reach a ledge that held a rude altar of piled stones, honoring the Wind God. He could see, not far below him, the Mountain Woman scrambling along, her red eyes blazing.

With a short prayer asking forgiveness for disturbing the altar, Minokichi pried the uppermost stone from the pile and sent the boulders rumbling down toward the ogress. She turned to run, but the huge stones overtook her and swept her off the mountain.

Wearily the woodcutter continued his climb. Night was falling, the wind was rising, and Minokichi was freezing. Soon it was so dark, he could no longer even see the trail.

Then a procession of fifty globes of bright white light floated up behind him. It seemed to be a procession of men carrying lanterns, but Minokichi soon realized they were ghost-lights, drifting by themselves, unmindful of the awful winds.

As the fiery globes drew near, Minokichi pressed himself against the side of the cliff, not daring to touch the eerie balls. But when the last one had passed him, he followed behind them, their light guiding him the rest of the way up the trail.

At the top they led him around jagged stones and through snowdrifts so deep that he could scarcely keep up. Despairingly he thought, Now I am certainly going to die.

Then far ahead he saw the fire-globes moving up a broad flight of snow-covered steps and entering a stone temple. By the time he reached the steps, all of the lights were inside, their brightness blazing through the open doors.

This must be the shrine of the Wind God, he thought as he forced his frozen legs to climb the stairs.

Inside he found the air warm, and he could no longer hear the howling wind. Nor could he see a single fire-globe. The whole place was now filled with a soft, pearly light that seemed to come from the very stones of the shrine.

Exhausted, he sank to his knees, leaning against one wall. It felt warm even through his coat. He closed his eyes for just a moment, lulled by the heat, and instantly fell asleep.

He awoke at dawn. The air and stone had grown chill; hissing snow was piling up in the open doorway. Pulling his coat tightly around him, Minokichi peered out at the driving snow.

Through the churning whiteness he saw a huge shape approaching—
at first just a dark blur touched with red and gold.

The storm slackened abruptly, then formed an enormous whirlwind
at the foot of the steps. Now Minokichi could see clearly a giant with
gleaming bluish skin, a mouth full of sharp white teeth, and eyes like
polished black stones. He wore breeches made from cloth-of-gold edged
in black and red. A red and gold scarf circled a neck as thick as a tree
trunk.

The giant lowered a huge sack to the ground. He untied the neck
and held it open. Instantly the whirlwind poured itself inside. Then the
Wind God (for Minokichi had no doubt that this was the god) retied
the bag.

Suddenly he turned to the woodcutter.

Minokichi sank to his knees and bowed low.

"How dare you enter my shrine," thundered the god, "after destroying
one of my altars!"

"I ask forgiveness. Circumstances—a white hairy ogress to be exact—
forced my disrespectful act," said Minokichi.

"You have made the path safer for those who come to honor me. For this unwitting—but useful—service, I forgive you. But why have you come?"

His voice shaking, Minokichi quickly explained about Yuki, his broken promise, and his desire to win back his wife.

"You cast away her chance to remain mortal," rumbled the Wind God. "Now she haunts the snows, doing my bidding."

"Return my wife to me," pleaded Minokichi, "and I promise we will raise a fine altar to you in our village. We will tend it, and our children, and our children's children."

"You broke one promise already," the Wind God grumbled.

"And as a result I have learned the value of keeping a promise," said Minokichi, "and the pain of breaking one."

"See that you keep your word," warned the other, opening his sack and freeing a wind that rushed away to the west.

In a short time the wind returned, driving the Woman of the Snow in front of it. Her garments of white trailed away to mist, her black hair streamed out in the wind, her arms of dazzling white reached out from her billowing kimono sleeves.

Minokichi felt dizzy with hope—then hopeless. In her cold eyes he saw no memory of him or the love they once shared.

"Why did your wind bring me here?" she asked, bowing before the Wind God. "I was flying toward some lost travelers. Surely they will have reached safety by now."

"I am turning you back into a mortal," the god said. "Go back to your family. But never let your husband forget his promise."

He vanished. On the expanse of snow and ice stood Yuki, her eyes glowing with the warmth of love and remembering.

Minokichi ran down the steps and embraced her.

When they returned to their village, they built an altar to the Wind God, which they tended, as did their children and their grandchildren, always faithful to the promise Minokichi had made to regain his beloved snow wife.